LETTER OF THE LAW

LETTER OF THE LAW

by Alan E. Nourse

The place was dark and damp, and smelled like moldy leaves. Meyerhoff followed the huge, bear-like Altairian guard down the slippery flagstones of the corridor, sniffing the dead, musty air with distaste. He drew his carefully tailored Terran-styled jacket closer about his shoulders, shivering as his eyes avoided the black, yawning cell-holes they were passing. His foot slipped on the slimy flags from time to time, and finally he paused to wipe the caked mud from his trouser leg. "How much farther is it?" he shouted angrily.

The guard waved a heavy paw vaguely into the blackness ahead. Quite suddenly the corridor took a sharp bend, and the Altairian stopped, producing a huge key ring from some obscure fold of his hairy hide. "I still don't see any reason for all the fuss," he grumbled in a wounded tone. "We've treated him like a brother."

One of the huge steel doors clicked open. Meyerhoff peered into the blackness, catching a vaguely human outline against the back wall. "Harry?" he called sharply.

There was a startled gasp from within, and a skinny, gnarled little man suddenly appeared in the guard's light, like a grotesque, twisted ghost out of the blackness. Wide blue eyes regarded Meyerhoff from beneath uneven black eyebrows, and then the little man's face broke into a crafty grin. "Paul! So they sent you! I knew I could count on it!" He executed a deep, awkward bow, motioning Meyerhoff into the dark cubicle. "Not much to offer you," he said slyly, "but it's the best I can do under the circumstances."

Meyerhoff scowled, and turned abruptly to the guard. "We'll have some privacy now, if you please. Interplanetary ruling. And leave us the light."

LETTER OF THE LAW

The guard grumbled, and started for the door. "It's about time you showed up!" cried the little man in the cell. "Great day! Lucky they sent you, pal. Why, I've been in here for years—"

"Look, Zeckler, the name is Meyerhoff, and I'm not your pal," Meyerhoff snapped. "And you've been here for two weeks, three days, and approximately four hours. You're getting as bad as your gentle guards when it comes to bandying the truth around." He peered through the dim light at the gaunt face of the prisoner. Zeckler's face was dark with a week's beard, and his bloodshot eyes belied the cocky grin on his lips. His clothes were smeared and sodden, streaked with great splotches of mud and moss. Meyerhoff's face softened a little. "So Harry Zeckler's in a jam again," he said. "You *look* as if they'd treated you like a brother."

The little man snorted. "These overgrown teddy-bears don't know what brotherhood means, nor humanity, either. Bread and water I've been getting, nothing more, and then only if they feel like bringing it down." He sank wearily down on the rock bench along the wall. "I thought you'd never get here! I sent an appeal to the Terran Consulate the first day I was arrested. What happened? I mean, all they had to do was get a man over here, get the extradition papers signed, and provide transportation off the planet for me. Why so much time? I've been sitting here rotting—" He broke off in mid-sentence and stared at Meyerhoff. "You *brought* the papers, didn't you? I mean, we can leave now?"

Meyerhoff stared at the little man with a mixture of pity and disgust. "You are a prize fool," he said finally. "Did you know that?"

Zeckler's eyes widened. "What do you mean, fool? So I spend a couple of weeks in this pneumonia trap. The deal was worth it! I've got three million credits sitting in the Terran Consulate on Altair V, just waiting for me to walk in and pick them up.

Three million credits—do you hear? That's enough to set me up for life!"

Meyerhoff nodded grimly. "*If* you live long enough to walk in and pick them up, that is."

"What do you mean, if?"

Meyerhoff sank down beside the man, his voice a tense whisper in the musty cell. "I mean that right now you are practically dead. You may not know it, but you are. You walk into a newly opened planet with your smart little bag of tricks, walk in here with a shaky passport and no permit, with no knowledge of the natives outside of two paragraphs of inaccuracies in the Explorer's Guide, and even then you're not content to come in and sell something legitimate, something the natives might conceivably be able to use. No, nothing so simple for you. You have to pull your usual high-pressure stuff. And this time, buddy, you're paying the piper."

"*You mean I'm not being extradited?*"

Meyerhoff grinned unpleasantly. "I mean precisely that. You've committed a crime here—a major crime. The Altairians are sore about it. And the Terran Consulate isn't willing to sell all the trading possibilities here down the river just to get you out of a mess. You're going to stand trial—and these natives are out to get you. Personally, I think they're *going* to get you."

Zeckler stood up shakily. "You can't believe anything the natives say," he said uneasily. "They're pathological liars. Why, you should see what they tried to sell *me*! You've never seen such a pack of liars as these critters." He glanced up at Meyerhoff. "They'll probably drop a little fine on me and let me go."

"A little fine of one Terran neck." Meyerhoff grinned nastily. "You've committed the most heinous crime these creatures can imagine, and they're going to get you for it if it's the last thing they do. I'm afraid, my friend, that your con-man days are over."

LETTER OF THE LAW

Zeckler fished in the other man's pocket, extracted a cigarette, and lighted it with trembling fingers. "It's bad, then," he said finally.

"It's bad, all right."

Some shadow of the sly, elfin grin crept over the little con-man's face. "Well, at any rate, I'm glad they sent you over," he said weakly. "Nothing like a good lawyer to handle a trial."

"*Lawyer?* Not me! Oh, no. Sorry, but no thanks." Meyerhoff chuckled. "I'm your advisor, old boy. Nothing else. I'm here to keep you from botching things up still worse for the Trading Commission, that's all. I wouldn't get tangled up in a mess with those creatures for anything!" He shook his head. "You're your own lawyer, Mr. Super-salesman. It's all your show. And you'd better get your head out of the sand, or you're going to lose a case like it's never been lost before!"

*

Meyerhoff watched the man's pale face, and shook his head. In a way, he thought, it was a pity to see such a change in the rosy-cheeked, dapper, cocksure little man who had talked his way glibly in and out of more jams than Meyerhoff could count. Trading brought scalpers; it was almost inevitable that where rich and unexploited trading ground was uncovered, it would first fall prey to the fast-trading boys. They spread out from Terra with the first wave of exploration—the slick, fast-talking con-men who could work new territories unfettered by the legal restrictions that soon closed down the more established planets. The first men in were the richest out, and through some curious quirk of the Terrestrial mind, they knew they could count on Terran protection, however crooked and underhand their methods.

But occasionally a situation arose where the civilization and social practices of the alien victims made it unwise to tamper with them. Altair I had been recognized at once by the Trading

Commission as a commercial prize of tremendous value, but early reports had warned of the danger of wildcat trading on the little, musty, jungle-like planet with its shaggy, three-eyed inhabitants—warned specifically against the confidence tactics so frequently used—but there was always somebody, Meyerhoff reflected sourly, who just didn't get the word.

Zeckler puffed nervously on his cigarette, his narrow face a study in troubled concentration. "But I didn't *do* anything!" he exploded finally. "So I pulled an old con game. So what? Why should they get so excited? So I clipped a few thousand credits, pulled a little fast business." He shrugged eloquently, spreading his hands. "Everybody's doing it. They do it to each other without batting an eye. You should *see* these critters operate on each other. Why, my little scheme was peanuts by comparison."

Meyerhoff pulled a pipe from his pocket, and began stuffing the bowl with infinite patience. "And precisely what sort of con game was it?" he asked quietly.

Zeckler shrugged again. "The simplest, tiredest, moldiest old racket that ever made a quick nickel. Remember the old Terran gag about the Brooklyn Bridge? The same thing. Only these critters didn't want bridges. They wanted land—this gooey, slimy swamp they call 'farm land.' So I gave them what they wanted. I just sold them some land."

Meyerhoff nodded fiercely. "You sure did. A hundred square kilos at a swipe. Only you sold the same hundred square kilos to a dozen different natives." Suddenly he threw back his hands and roared. "Of all the things you *shouldn't* have done—"

"But what's a chunk of land?"

Meyerhoff shook his head hopelessly. "If you hadn't been so greedy, you'd have found out what a chunk of land was to these natives before you started peddling it. You'd have found out other things about them, too. You'd have learned that in spite of all their bumbling and fussing and squabbling they're not so

9

dull. You'd have found out that they're marsupials, and that two out of five of them get thrown out of their mother's pouch before they're old enough to survive. You'd have realized that they have to start fighting for individual rights almost as soon as they're born. Anything goes, as long as it benefits them as individuals."

Meyerhoff grinned at the little man's horrified face. "Never heard of that, had you? And you've never heard of other things, too. You've probably never heard that there are just too many Altairians here for the food their planet can supply, and their diet is so finicky that they just can't live on anything that doesn't grow here. And consequently, land is the key factor in their economy, not money; nothing but land. To get land, it's every man for himself, and the loser starves, and their entire legal and monetary system revolves on that principle. They've built up the most confusing and impossible system of barter and trade imaginable, aimed at individual survival, with land as the value behind the credit. That explains the lying—of course they're liars, with an economy like that. They've completely missed the concept of truth. Pathological? You bet they're pathological! Only a fool would tell the truth when his life depended on his being a better liar than the next guy! Lying is the time-honored tradition, with their entire legal system built around it."

Zeckler snorted. "But how could they *possibly* have a legal system? I mean, if they don't recognize the truth when it slaps them in the face?"

Meyerhoff shrugged. "As we understand legal systems, I suppose they don't have one. They have only the haziest idea what truth represents, and they've shrugged off the idea as impossible and useless." He chuckled maliciously. "So you went out and found a chunk of ground in the uplands, and sold it to a dozen separate, self-centered, half-starved natives!

Encroachment on private property is legal grounds for murder on this planet, and twelve of them descended on the same chunk of land at the same time, all armed with title-deeds." Meyerhoff sighed. "You've got twelve mad Altairians in your hair. You've got a mad planet in your hair. And in the meantime, Terra's most valuable uranium source in five centuries is threatening to cut off supply unless they see your blood splattered liberally all the way from here to the equator."

Zeckler was visibly shaken. "Look," he said weakly, "so I wasn't so smart. What am I going to do? I mean, are you going to sit quietly by and let them butcher me? How could I defend myself in a legal setup like *this?*"

Meyerhoff smiled coolly. "You're going to get your sly little con-man brain to working, I think," he said softly. "By Interplanetary Rules, they have to give you a trial in Terran legal form—judge, jury, court procedure, all that folderol. They think it's a big joke—after all, what could a judicial oath mean to them?—but they agreed. Only thing is, they're going to hang you, if they die trying. So you'd better get those stunted little wits of yours clicking—and if you try to implicate *me*, even a little bit, I'll be out of there so fast you won't know what happened."

With that Meyerhoff walked to the door. He jerked it inward sharply, and spilled two guards over on their faces. "Privacy," he grunted, and started back up the slippery corridor.

*

It certainly *looked* like a courtroom, at any rate. In the front of the long, damp stone room was a bench, with a seat behind it, and a small straight chair to the right. To the left was a stand with twelve chairs—larger chairs, with a railing running along the front. The rest of the room was filled almost to the door with seats facing the bench. Zeckler followed the shaggy-haired guard into the room, nodding approvingly. "Not such a bad arrangement," he said. "They must have gotten the idea fast."

Meyerhoff wiped the perspiration from his forehead, and shot the little con-man a stony glance. "At least you've got a courtroom, a judge, and a jury for this mess. Beyond that—" He shrugged eloquently. "I can't make any promises."

In the back of the room a door burst open with a bang. Loud, harsh voices were heard as half a dozen of the huge Altairians attempted to push through the door at once. Zeckler clamped on the headset to his translator unit, and watched the hubbub in the anteroom with growing alarm. Finally the question of precedent seemed to be settled, and a group of the Altairians filed in, in order of stature, stalking across the room in flowing black robes, pug-nosed faces glowering with self-importance. They descended upon the jury box, grunting and scrapping with each other for the first-row seats, and the judge took his place with obvious satisfaction behind the heavy wooden bench. Finally, the prosecuting attorney appeared, flanked by two clerks, who took their places beside him. The prosecutor eyed Zeckler with cold malevolence, then turned and delivered a sly wink at the judge.

In a moment the room was a hubbub as it filled with the huge, bumbling, bear-like creatures, jostling each other and fighting for seats, growling and complaining. Two small fights broke out in the rear, but were quickly subdued by the group of gendarmes guarding the entrance. Finally the judge glared down at Zeckler with all three eyes, and pounded the bench top with a wooden mallet until the roar of activity subsided. The jurymen wriggled uncomfortably in their seats, exchanging winks, and finally turned their attention to the front of the court.

"We are reading the case of the people of Altair I," the judge's voice roared out, "against one Harry Zeckler—" he paused for a long, impressive moment—"Terran." The courtroom immediately burst into an angry growl, until the judge pounded the bench five or six times more. "This—creature—is hereby accused of the following crimes," the judge bellowed. "Conspiracy to overthrow the government of Altair I. Brutal murder of seventeen law-abiding citizens of the village of Karzan at the third hour before dawn in the second period after his arrival. Desecration of the Temple of our beloved Goddess Zermat, Queen of the Harvest. Conspiracy with the lesser gods to cause the unprecedented drought in the Dermatti section of our fair globe. Obscene exposure of his pouch-marks in a public square. Four separate and distinct charges of jail-break and bribery—" The judge pounded the bench for order—"Espionage with the accursed scum of Altair II in preparation for interplanetary invasion."

The little con-man's jaw sagged lower and lower, the color draining from his face. He turned, wide-eyed, to Meyerhoff, then back to the judge.

"The Chairman of the Jury," said the Judge succinctly, "will read the verdict."

The little native in the front of the jury-box popped up like a puppet on a string. "Defendant found guilty on all counts," he said.

"Defendant is guilty! The court will pronounce sentence—"

"*Now wait a minute!*" Zeckler was on his feet, wild-eyed. "What kind of railroad job—"

The judge blinked disappointedly at Paul Meyerhoff. "Not yet?" he asked, unhappily.

"No." Meyerhoff's hands twitched nervously. "Not yet, Your Honor. Later, Your Honor. The trial comes *first*."

The judge looked as if his candy had been stolen. "But you *said* I should call for the verdict."

"Later. You have to have the trial before you can have the verdict."

LETTER OF THE LAW

The Altairian shrugged indifferently. "Now—later—" he muttered.

"Have the prosecutor call his first witness," said Meyerhoff.

Zeckler leaned over, his face ashen. "These charges," he whispered. "They're insane!"

"Of course they are," Meyerhoff whispered back.

"But what am I going to—"

"Sit tight. Let *them* set things up."

"But those *lies*. They're liars, the whole pack of them—" He broke off as the prosecutor roared a name.

The shaggy brute who took the stand was wearing a bright purple hat which sat rakishly over one ear. He grinned the Altairian equivalent of a hungry grin at the prosecutor. Then he cleared his throat and started. "This Terran riffraff—"

"The oath," muttered the judge. "We've got to have the oath."

The prosecutor nodded, and four natives moved forward, carrying huge inscribed marble slabs to the front of the court. One by one the chunks were reverently piled in a heap at the witness's feet. The witness placed a huge, hairy paw on the cairn, and the prosecutor said, "Do you swear to tell the truth, the whole truth, and nothing but the truth, so help you—" he paused to squint at the paper in his hand, and finished on a puzzled note, "—Goddess?"

The witness removed the paw from the rock pile long enough to scratch his ear. Then he replaced it, and replied, "Of course," in an injured tone.

"Then tell this court what you have seen of the activities of this abominable wretch."

The witness settled back into the chair, fixing one eye on Zeckler's face, another on the prosecutor, and closing the third as if in meditation. "I think it happened on the fourth night of the seventh crossing of Altair II (may the Goddess cast a drought upon it)—or was it the seventh night of the fourth crossing?—" he grinned apologetically at the judge—"when I was making my way back through town toward my blessed land-plot, minding my own business, Your Honor, after weeks of bargaining for the crop I was harvesting. Suddenly from the shadow of the building, this creature—" he waved a paw at Zeckler—"stopped me in my tracks with a vicious cry. He had a weapon I'd never seen before, and before I could find my voice he forced me back against the wall. I could see by the cruel glint in his eyes that there was no warmth, no sympathy in his heart, that I was—"

"Objection!" Zeckler squealed plaintively, jumping to his feet. "This witness can't even remember what night he's talking about!"

The judge looked startled. Then he pawed feverishly through his bundle of notes. "Overruled," he said abruptly. "Continue, please."

The witness glowered at Zeckler. "As I was saying before this loutish interruption," he muttered, "I could see that I was face to face with the most desperate of criminal types, even for Terrans. Note the shape of his head, the flabbiness of his ears. I was petrified with fear. And then, helpless as I was, this two-legged abomination began to shower me with threats of evil to my blessed home, dark threats of poisoning my land unless I would tell him where he could find the resting place of our blessed Goddess—"

"I never saw him before in my life," Zeckler moaned to Meyerhoff. "Listen to him! Why should I care where their Goddess—"

Meyerhoff gave him a stony look. "The Goddess runs things around here. She makes it rain. If it doesn't rain, somebody's insulted her. It's very simple."

"But how can I fight testimony like that?"

LETTER OF THE LAW

"I doubt if you *can* fight it."

"But they can't prove a word of it—" He looked at the jury, who were listening enraptured to the second witness on the stand. This one was testifying regarding the butcherous slaughter of eighteen (or was it twenty-three? Oh, yes, twenty-three) women and children in the suburban village of Karzan. The pogrom, it seemed, had been accomplished by an energy weapon which ate great, gaping holes in the sides of buildings. A third witness took the stand, continuing the drone as the room grew hotter and muggier. Zeckler grew paler and paler, his eyes turning glassy as the testimony piled up. "But it's not *true*," he whispered to Meyerhoff.

"Of course it isn't! Can't you understand? *These people have no regard for truth.* It's stupid, to them, silly, a mark of low intelligence. The only thing in the world they have any respect for is a liar bigger and more skillful than they are."

Zeckler jerked around abruptly as he heard his name bellowed out. "Does the defendant have anything to say before the jury delivers the verdict?"

"Do I have—" Zeckler was across the room in a flash, his pale cheeks suddenly taking on a feverish glow. He sat down gingerly on the witness chair, facing the judge, his eyes bright with fear and excitement. "Your—Your Honor, I—I have a statement to make which will have a most important bearing on this case. You must listen with the greatest care." He glanced quickly at Meyerhoff, and back to the judge. "Your Honor," he said in a hushed voice. "You are in gravest of danger. All of you. Your lives—your very land is at stake."

The judge blinked, and shuffled through his notes hurriedly as a murmur arose in the court. "Our land?"

"Your lives, your land, everything you hold dear," Zeckler said quickly, licking his lips nervously. "You must try to understand me—" he glanced apprehensively over his shoulder "now,

16

because I may not live long enough to repeat what I am about to tell you—"

The murmur quieted down, all ears straining in their headsets to hear his words. "These charges," he continued, "all of them—they're perfectly true. At least, they *seem* to be perfectly true. But in every instance, I was working with heart and soul, risking my life, for the welfare of your beautiful planet."

There was a loud hiss from the back of the court. Zeckler frowned and rubbed his hands together. "It was my misfortune," he said, "to go to the wrong planet when I first came to Altair from my homeland on Terra. I—I landed on Altair II, a grave mistake, but as it turned out, a very fortunate error. Because in attempting to arrange trading in that frightful place, I made certain contacts." His voice trembled, and sank lower. "I learned the horrible thing which is about to happen to this planet, at the hands of those barbarians. The conspiracy is theirs, not mine. They have bribed your Goddess, flattered her and lied to her, coerced her all-powerful goodness to their own evil interests, preparing for the day when they could persuade her to cast your land into the fiery furnace of a ten-year-drought—"

Somebody in the middle of the court burst out laughing. One by one the natives nudged one another, and booed, and guffawed, until the rising tide of racket drowned out Zeckler's words. "The defendant is obviously lying," roared the prosecutor over the pandemonium. "Any fool knows that the Goddess can't be bribed. How could she be a Goddess if she could?"

Zeckler grew paler. "But—perhaps they were very clever—"

"And how could they flatter her, when she knows, beyond doubt, that she is the most exquisitely radiant creature in all the Universe? And *you* dare to insult her, drag her name in the dirt."

17

LETTER OF THE LAW

The hisses grew louder, more belligerent. Cries of "Butcher him!" and "Scald his bowels!" rose from the courtroom. The judge banged for silence, his eyes angry.

"Unless the defendant wishes to take up more of our precious time with these ridiculous lies, the jury—"

"Wait! Your Honor, I request a short recess before I present my final plea."

"Recess?"

"A few moments to collect my thoughts, to arrange my case."

The judge settled back with a disgusted snarl. "Do I have to?" he asked Meyerhoff.

Meyerhoff nodded. The judge shrugged, pointing over his shoulder to the anteroom. "You can go in there," he said.

Somehow, Zeckler managed to stumble from the witness stand, amid riotous boos and hisses, and tottered into the anteroom.

*

Zeckler puffed hungrily on a cigarette, and looked up at Meyerhoff with haunted eyes. "It—it doesn't look so good," he muttered.

Meyerhoff's eyes were worried, too. For some reason, he felt a surge of pity and admiration for the haggard con-man. "It's worse than I'd anticipated," he admitted glumly. "That was a good try, but you just don't know enough about them and their Goddess." He sat down wearily. "I don't see what you can do. They want your blood, and they're going to have it. They just won't believe you, no matter *how* big a lie you tell."

Zeckler sat in silence for a moment. "This lying business," he said finally, "exactly how does it work?"

"The biggest, most convincing liar wins. It's as simple as that. It doesn't matter how outlandish a whopper you tell. Unless, of course, they've made up their minds that you just naturally aren't as big a liar as they are. And it looks like that's just what

18

they've done. It wouldn't make any difference to them *what* you say—unless, somehow, you could *make* them believe it."

Zeckler frowned. "And how do they regard the—the biggest liar? I mean, how do they feel toward him?"

Meyerhoff shifted uneasily. "It's hard to say. It's been my experience that they respect him highly—maybe even fear him a little. After all, the most convincing liar always wins in any transaction, so he gets more land, more food, more power. Yes, I think the biggest liar could go where he pleased without any interference."

Zeckler was on his feet, his eyes suddenly bright with excitement. "Wait a minute," he said tensely. "To tell them a lie that they'd have to believe—a lie they simply couldn't *help* but believe—" He turned on Meyerhoff, his hands trembling. "Do they *think* the way we do? I mean, with logic, cause and effect, examining evidence and drawing conclusions? Given certain evidence, would they have to draw the same conclusions that we have to draw?"

Meyerhoff blinked. "Well—yes. Oh, yes, they're perfectly logical."

Zeckler's eyes flashed, and a huge grin broke out on his sallow face. His thin body fairly shook. He started hopping up and down on one foot, staring idiotically into space. "If I could only think—" he muttered. "Somebody—somewhere—something I read."

"Whatever are you talking about?"

"It was a Greek, I think—"

Meyerhoff stared at him. "Oh, come now. Have you gone off your rocker completely? You've got a problem on your hands, man."

"No, no, I've got a problem in the bag!" Zeckler's cheeks flushed. "Let's go back in there—I think I've got an answer!"

LETTER OF THE LAW

The courtroom quieted the moment they opened the door, and the judge banged the gavel for silence. As soon as Zeckler had taken his seat on the witness stand, the judge turned to the head juryman. "Now, then," he said with happy finality. "The jury—"

"Hold on! Just one minute more."

The judge stared down at Zeckler as if he were a bug on a rock. "Oh, yes. You had something else to say. Well, go ahead and say it."

Zeckler looked sharply around the hushed room. "You want to convict me," he said softly, "in the worst sort of way. Isn't that right?"

Eyes swung toward him. The judge broke into an evil grin. "That's right."

"But you can't really convict me until you've considered carefully any statement I make in my own defense. Isn't that right?"

The judge looked uncomfortable. "If you've got something to say, go ahead and say it."

"I've got just one statement to make. Short and sweet. But you'd better listen to it, and think it out carefully before you decide that you really want to convict me." He paused, and glanced slyly at the judge. "You don't think much of those who tell the truth, it seems. Well, put *this* statement in your record, then." His voice was loud and clear in the still room. "*All Earthmen are absolutely incapable of telling the truth.*"

Puzzled frowns appeared on the jury's faces. One or two exchanged startled glances, and the room was still as death. The judge stared at him, and then at Meyerhoff, then back. "But you"—he stammered. "You're"—He stopped in mid-sentence, his jaw sagging.

20

One of the jurymen let out a little squeak, and fainted dead away. It took, all in all, about ten seconds for the statement to soak in.

And then pandemonium broke loose in the courtroom.

*

"Really," said Harry Zeckler loftily, "it was so obvious I'm amazed that it didn't occur to me first thing." He settled himself down comfortably in the control cabin of the Interplanetary Rocket and grinned at the outline of Altair IV looming larger in the view screen.

Paul Meyerhoff stared stonily at the controls, his lips compressed angrily. "You might at least have told me what you were planning."

"And take the chance of being overheard? Don't be silly. It had to come as a bombshell. I had to establish myself as a liar—the prize liar of them all, but I had to tell the sort of lie that they simply could not cope with. Something that would throw them into such utter confusion that they wouldn't *dare* convict me." He grinned impishly at Meyerhoff. "The paradox of Epimenides the Cretan. It really stopped them cold. They *knew* I was an Earthmen, which meant that my statement that Earthmen were liars was a lie, which meant that maybe I wasn't a liar, in which case—oh, it was tailor-made."

"It sure was." Meyerhoff's voice was a snarl.

"Well, it made me out a liar in a class they couldn't approach, didn't it?"

Meyerhoff's face was purple with anger. "Oh, indeed it did! And it put *all* Earthmen in exactly the same class, too."

"So what's honor among thieves? I got off, didn't I?"

Meyerhoff turned on him fiercely. "Oh, you got off just fine. You scared the living daylights out of them. And in an eon of lying they never have run up against a short-circuit like that. You've also completely botched any hope of ever setting up a trading alliance with Altair I, and that includes uranium, too. Smart people don't gamble with loaded dice. You scared them so badly they don't want anything to do with us."

Zeckler's grin broadened, and he leaned back luxuriously. "Ah, well. After all, the Trading Alliance was *your* outlook, wasn't it? What a pity!" He clucked his tongue sadly. "Me, I've got a fortune in credits sitting back at the consulate waiting for me—enough to keep me on silk for quite a while, I might say. I think I'll just take a nice, long vacation."

Meyerhoff turned to him, and a twinkle of malignant glee appeared in his eyes. "Yes, I think you will. I'm quite sure of it, in fact. Won't cost you a cent, either."

"Eh?"

Meyerhoff grinned unpleasantly. He brushed an imaginary lint fleck from his lapel, and looked up at Zeckler slyly. "That—uh—jury trial. The Altairians weren't any too happy to oblige. They wanted to execute you outright. Thought a trial was awfully silly—until they got their money back, of course. Not too much—just three million credits."

Zeckler went white. "But that money was in banking custody!"

"Is that right? My goodness. You don't suppose they could have lost those papers, do you?" Meyerhoff grinned at the little con-man. "And incidentally, you're under arrest, you know."

A choking sound came from Zeckler's throat. "*Arrest!*"

"Oh, yes. Didn't I tell you? Conspiring to undermine the authority of the Terran Trading Commission. Serious charge, you know. Yes, I think we'll take a nice long vacation together, straight back to Terra. And there I think you'll face a jury trial."

Zeckler spluttered. "There's no evidence—you've got nothing on me! What kind of a frame are you trying to pull?"

"A *lovely* frame. Airtight. A frame from the bottom up, and you're right square in the middle. And this time—" Meyerhoff tapped a cigarette on his thumb with happy finality—"this time I *don't* think you'll get off."

www.ingramcontent.com/pod-product-compliance
Lightning Source LLC
Chambersburg PA
CBHW050921120626
46552CB00004B/1695